REVENGER

REVENGER

HE IS THE SHADOW IN YOUR DREAMS

Andrew Dennis Biersack

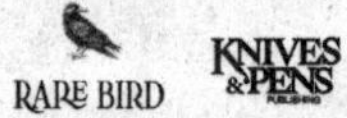

THIS IS A GENUINE RARE BIRD AND KNIVES & PENS BOOK

Rare Bird Books | Knives & Pens Publishing
6044 North Figueroa Street
Los Angeles, California 90042
rarebirdbooks.com

FIRST MASS MARKET EDITION

For more information, address:
Rare Bird Books Subsidiary Rights Department
6044 North Figueroa Street
Los Angeles, California 90042

Creative director/cover art by Brandon Stecz

Set in Dante

Printed in the United States

ISBN-13: 9781644284902

10 9 8 7 6 5 4 3 2 1

Library of Congress Cataloging-in-Publication Data
available upon request

1

THE WORLD IS BLEEDING

This infamous part of Manhattan was especially harsh in the 1980s.

In the shadowy underside of New York City, beneath the thin veneer of civilization, the clogged arteries of Hell's Kitchen pulsed with menace—tunnels filled with the scent of blood and urine. Fluorescent bulbs flickered like the last neurons of a dying god. This dimly lit subway platform had been left to its own devices. Decay followed. A stenchy urban jungle best tread through quickly.

Above, the city's tragedies played out under the streetlights.

Down here, the damned vanished into the dark.

The Revenger waited in the shadowy space between two pillars, a silhouette cloaked in matte black. Anyone who might've detected his outline wouldn't suspect that the shadows concealed a tailored black trench coat over a smart three-piece suit. His sharp facial features were seemingly always covered by the dark, his piercing steel-gray eyes staring out through the black. The crimson pocket square tucked into his coat was the only splash of color—a symbol of the blood fueling his unrelenting mission. His gloves were smooth leather, his rugged yet simple combat boots complementing his utilitarian style.

Inside the coat were his favorite tools: a pair of pistols customized for precision and silence, a stiletto dagger with a blackened steel blade designed for close combat, and a handful of throwing knives. All of these, of course, paled in comparison to his ability to wield the shadows themselves, manipulating them into tendrils of singular purpose.

Tonight's targets were about to feel the icy touch of all the Revenger commanded.

A clock on the wall ticked toward two in the morning. The last uptown train had already left, leaving only the gurgle of water in the drains and the occasional skitter of rat claws across tile. But something else moved in the station: a trio of rough-looking, middle-aged men shuffling down from the service entrance at the far end of the platform. Their laughter was thick, slurred by vodka and the excitement of a quick payday. They were Russian heavies, none of them "made," but all working for organized crime.

These half-drunk brawlers trafficked in both narcotics and human beings.

As one kept lookout, the other two approached a metal trash can in a dark corner and carefully retrieved the hidden cargo awaiting them: a small wooden crate tucked at the bottom. One of them pulled a crowbar from his tacky leather trench coat and forced open the lid. Inside, foam padding shifted to reveal bricks of powder, each wrapped in plastic. Satisfied with their inspection, one of them lifted the box, and they waited for a train.

Above them, the station lights flickered. A wave of darkness swept along the platform as two tubes failed, leaving only the sickly glow of a third. The Revenger watched the men squint, momentarily thrown off balance. He exhaled slowly. The sound insect-like, nearly swallowed by the ambient static of the city's quiet hours.

The Revenger blinked. For a moment, everything around him shimmered, a transparent layer revealing a decade's worth of hell. He saw jagged fragments of what he remembered as a staged robbery: the shooter's eyes wide with cruel certainty, the .38 delivering its message into the Revenger's side, a second shot, a woman's hand as it slipped from his. His wife? Who was the Revenger before he became…this?

In another instant, he snapped back to reality—and to his mission.

He crept along the perimeter, using the flickering light as both cover and rhythm—each flash a signal, each shadow an invitation.

The lookout stood at the edge of the track, face turned away, shoulders hunched. His cigarette was a brief, trembling spark. As the Revenger stealthily approached, the shadow behind him grew larger than it had any natural right to be.

The darkness peeled off the wall behind him and wrapped around the lookout's neck.

The man gasped, trying to scream, but only a strangled squeak escaped before the quick snap.

The Revenger pulled the lifeless body back between the pillars and laid it down as carefully as one can place a fresh corpse.

Two remained. The Revenger stayed in the shadows, listening to them argue with each other in Russian. What mattered wasn't their words but rather their choreography: the hands, the stance, how one leaned against a column while the other paced in tight circles.

He waited for the moment when the leaning man looked away, toward the stairwell, searching the dark for the missing lookout. The Revenger plunged his stiletto dagger into the man's kidneys and stomach in rapid motions, finishing with a final stab to the jugular. The man thrashed, kicked, and the crate toppled, bricks of heroin spilling onto the dirty tile. The last man turned, hand on the grip of a pistol, but he was too late.

The Revenger let the body fall, then stood still, as if daring the last thug to look at him. For a moment, the two were frozen in place: the trafficker, gun raised, hands trembling; and the vigilante, silent and unblinking.

"You aren't sneaking up on me," the man said, attempting to convince himself he'd regained his confidence and composure. "And I've got a gun, pal."

The man grinned. "Do you know whose dope you're stealing?"

The Revenger didn't move.

"Guess you'll never know, because you'll be dead."

He fired three shots, deafening in the tight space. Impossibly, he missed, the bullets seemingly swallowed by the shadows themselves. Now it was the Revenger who smiled.

The lone gunman dropped his pistol and fled.

The Revenger calmly watched him run. He surveyed the chaos: two bodies, one crate, and the faint smell of blood wafting into the humid air.

Slava, as he was called, did not run far. He cowered by a pay phone at the platform's far end, a switchblade clutched in both hands.

Western Electric had made these wall-mounted Bell pay phones heavy, but they offered no protection on this night.

The Revenger advanced with the inevitability of death itself. His boots squeaked on the wet tile. The lights stuttered overhead, alternately bleaching and erasing his silhouette. Even when the fluorescents surged, the shadows seemed reluctant to part from his outline. They pooled beneath his coat, oozed out between his fingers.

"Who are you?" Slava demanded, voice torn between rage and terror. His accent thickened around the consonants, rendering the words half-slurred, half-spat.

The Revenger said nothing. He only looked at Slava, head tilted with the cold curiosity of a biologist examining a twitching insect.

Slava stabbed wildly in the direction of the Revenger, who sidestepped so fluidly that it seemed he vanished and reappeared with each motion.

He seized Slava's wrists and twisted. There was a soft, wet pop—shoulders unseating from sockets—and a shriek that rebounded off the walls. With his next motion, the Revenger brought an elbow down on the man's clavicle. Bone shattered.

For an instant, the two locked eyes as the switchblade clattered.

The Revenger gripped Slava by the face—thumb in one cheek, fingers in the other. He squeezed. The jaw dislocated with a wet snap. The Revenger pulled him over the pay phone partition and slammed his head against the coin box. Once. Twice.

He dragged each body to a pillar and arranged them carefully; each corpse sat against the column, their dead eyes open.

At the far wall, a graffiti mural sagged beneath decades of grime. Beneath it, a blank panel of tile glared out, unspoiled, as if awaiting inscription. The Revenger knelt by the closest corpse and pressed two fingers into the sticky dark of the pooling blood. He smeared it on his gloved hand, then rose to face the wall.

He began to write, each letter deliberate, as if he were carving epitaphs rather than painting in gore. The message unspooled in block capitals:

YOUR SIN WILL SET ME FREE

He paused after the "N," his hand hovering over the wet tile. The blood on his glove gleamed in the failing light. For an instant, the station blurred at the edges—a faint overlay of memory, of a childhood spent in churches where incense mingled with candlewax, a face glimpsed through firelight.

The tremor in his hand surprised him. It lasted only a second, but it was enough. He clenched his fist, crushed the moment into nothing, and finished the message.

A final period, a crimson dot.

He stepped back and admired his work, tilting his head the way a craftsman does when evaluating a finished piece. The world snapped back into focus, hard and cold.

The Revenger turned away from the wall and strode into the gloom of the maintenance corridor—a one-eyed alley cat, fur matted by rain, slunk down the stairwell.

It paused, ears canted, and surveyed the carnage with the blank patience of its kind. The animal stepped delicately around the congealing puddles, nose twitching, then licked at the blood with a rough pink tongue.

Its left eye—milky, useless—stared straight at the wall, as if it understood.

The cat lingered a while, then melted into the darkness, following the same impossible path as the Revenger.

For a while, only the low buzz of the flickering lights broke the silence.

Then, with a groan of machinery, the next train arrived, its doors opening onto the empty station, followed by the screams of its jaded but stunned passengers.

2

THE WOUNDS I'VE MADE

Eleanor Kane crouched at the edge of the platform, notebook balanced on her thigh, voice recorder clicking softly in her left hand. The air was humid and stinking of bleach, though it barely masked the older, heavier smell beneath—iron, rot, and damp concrete.

The area echoed with the shuffle of detectives and the buzz of fluorescent tubes struggling to illuminate the space. She mostly ignored the uniforms standing to her right, their bulk blocking out the little light that filtered down from the bulbs overhead.

The cops knew her. They didn't always love her reporting, but they respected her sharp eye for details others overlooked.

"Victims?" she asked, not looking up.

"Three males," said a uniform behind her. "Found about two hours ago. Locals heard gunfire, but by the time Transit responded…"

He trailed off, gesturing to the pillars.

Eleanor didn't need him to finish. She'd already seen the bodies: posed against the columns, eyes open, throats cut. The message written on the far wall bled down the tile in brown streaks.

She clicked STOP on the recorder, rewound, then hit RECORD again.

"Three adult males, Caucasian, mid-thirties to forties," she said in her calm monotone. "Multiple stab wounds, bodies arranged postmortem. Message in blood on east wall reads: 'YOUR SIN WILL SET ME FREE.'"

The uniform shifted behind her, muttering something about the press being vultures. She ignored him. The cops didn't love her, but they knew better than to move her along. Her stories made them look competent.

She snapped a Polaroid, waited for the mechanical whine, then took another. The flash briefly turned the tiled walls into a morgue of white rectangles. She labeled the prints in neat block letters.

She stepped closer to the writing on the wall. The blood had begun to congeal, but the lettering was deliberate—each stroke confident, controlled. This wasn't graffiti.

This was a sermon.

"Same hand as the Rivington case," she muttered into the recorder. "Consistent pressure, same height, same angle of descent. Perp shows ritual precision."

She crouched again, tracing the pattern of footprints near the bloodstains—heavy soles, deep tread, military issue by the look of it. As she straightened, the camera strap slid from her shoulder and clattered against the floor. She didn't flinch.

She stood, her knees cracking loudly, and walked slowly in a tight circle around the bodies, keeping her distance. She set the camera down, then fished a Sharpie from her bag, labeling the white frames with her precise block capitals.

The uniform spoke again. "Have you seen this kind of thing before?"

Eleanor looked up, her face unreadable. "Twice," she said.

She tilted her head, mentally mapping out the force, the height, and the motion sequence. She closed her notebook with a soft snap, then flicked off the voice recorder.

Eleanor slung her camera over her shoulder and tucked the notebook into her jacket. As she ascended the stairs into the sour-smelling air, she paused at the curb to check her notes in the early morning sun. She reviewed the details, cross-referencing them with patterns from other cases, and felt the familiar chill: this was connected. It had to be.

She began walking, carefully avoiding the puddles, her mind calculating her next move as she blended into the city's flow. Behind her, sirens wailed, and the windows on the block lit up with flashing blue and red. But Eleanor moved through it unbothered, already halfway to her next destination.

That evening, elsewhere, Father Elias knelt before the altar, knees pressed deeply into the worn velvet cushion, hands folded in a gesture just shy of prayer. The nave of Saint Mark's was a cathedral only by license—a centuries-old Lithuanian parish recycled multiple times, patched and mended, its rafters cobwebbed and its columns reinforced with chicken wire and tar. The only light came from the candles on the altar and from the match Elias struck, trembling in his fingers before he touched it to the waiting wick.

The flame flickered, then steadied, illuminating the salt-and-pepper stubble on his jaw, the deep grooves in his cheeks, and the bloodless cracks on his lips. He watched the flame move down, licking the pale wax, before placing the taper in a battered brass holder. He repeated the motion slowly and deliberately, like a man paying penance inch by inch.

Elias pressed a thin, black-bound prayer book against his chest, its once-white edges faded to ash and smudged from decades of use. The words inside were burned into his mind, but he mouthed them anyway, voice barely audible over the whisper of drafts slipping through the apse.

He prayed for mercy, though he doubted it would come.

From the transept, the organ emitted a single, queasy note—the residue of a breeze through a cracked pipe. Elias did not flinch. He had spent so many nights in this church awake, that the usual creep of fear no longer applied. What kept him awake was a different kind of dread: the knowledge that out there, in the dark, were Satan's helpers.

He finished lighting the candles and stood, his joints protesting. He placed the prayer book on the altar, fingers resting on its cover, and looked up at the stained glass above the nave. Even at night, with the city's neon failing to pierce the soot on the glass, the colors shone through a shattered Madonna, her arms cracked by a split.

He turned and let his eyes scan the pews. They were empty, as always, but he imagined the old regulars: Mrs. Kowalczyk, who had confessed every Friday for twenty years and whose son was now in Sing Sing; Mr. Russo, shot in the knee by a loan shark but still insistent on kneeling during Mass; and the rest, all shadows in their faded Sunday best, all hoping for absolution from a priest who could barely grant it to himself.

He walked the length of the nave, footsteps echoing off the cracked tile. At the end, he paused to examine a broken statue of Saint Michael. The angel's sword had been snapped off, its face chipped and pockmarked, but the eyes—flat and expressionless—seemed to watch him. Elias reached out and traced a finger along the break, feeling the rough edge where violence had left its mark.

He lit another match and touched it to a fresh votive at the base of the statue.

"Forgive them," he whispered. "Though they know exactly what they do."

The phrase sounded empty. He'd used it before, for the man called the Revenger, years ago, when he first came to confession. Elias had heard all kinds of sins, but these always seemed to come with a sense of inevitability, as if the Revenger followed a script.

Father Elias had warned him then: vengeance would consume him.

He wandered into the sacristy, its walls close and smelling of wet stone and candlewax.

He took off his cassock, hung it on the battered hook, and ran water over his hands, scrubbing until his skin was raw. He dried them on his shirt, then slumped onto a pew. He grabbed a cigarette from the desk drawer, lit it, and exhaled into the gloom.

3

NO MERCY LEFT

The few cops who might have shown up at Club Euphoria this late were more interested in scoring than policing. The service entrance was a battered rectangle of rusted steel, covered with gum and the scorched remnants of a dozen previous lock jobs. The door caved in from the force of the Revenger's shoulder with a snap, hinges wheezing as it opened onto a corridor. The corridor smelled of fryer oil and cheap industrial solvent, a tang that masked, but did not erase, the stench of booze and sweat.

Adrian Vale ran Club Euphoria. Young, thin, pale, and handsome, he spoke softly, as if every word were a secret. Vale's effortless charm and magnetism put runaways, junkies, and low-level thugs at ease. He was a captain for the Syndicate, the city's fearsome secret society of seasoned criminals, and the primary target of the Revenger's ire.

The Revenger regarded Vale as a false idol, a corrupt dealer whose only loyalty was to desire itself. Vale symbolized the decade's obsessions, compulsions, and cravings—its hedonism and cocaine culture, its seductive recklessness.

The Revenger moved down the hall. He wore his now recognizable outfit. His face resembled a geometry problem: the sharp lines of his jaw and brow cast shadows, and the skin beneath his eyes was pale and tight. He kept his head lowered and his breath shallow, pausing only to listen to the muffled beat of the bass and the thumping of bodies.

The corridor ended at a mesh door. Behind it, he could see the club's main floor—a chaos of heat and violence pulsing to the beat of Pat Benatar's "Love Is a Battlefield," all painted in the harsh glows of pink and blue strobes.

The crowd moved as one: boys with razor-sharp haircuts and girls in Mylar skirts, their bodies gleaming with sweat from amphetamines and joyless sex, all orbiting the club's central pit. Above the pit was the catwalk, a grated walkway hung by steel chains and decorated with Christmas lights, where VIPs and security watched the chaos from above like gods who had misplaced their shame.

The Revenger slipped through the mesh onto the catwalk, his boots silent on the grate. He crouched, letting the light cast wild, alternating stripes across his coat and face. From this angle, he had a clear view of the bar—bartenders in sequined vests sliding drinks down the mirror-polished counter, their arms decorated with fluorescent bracelets. He counted the exits. Two real ones, both guarded by patches of muscle in nylon jackets. A third, poorly disguised as a staff-only door, led directly to where he'd parked his car.

The catwalk swayed as he moved closer to the control booth. He found the breaker panel tucked behind a rack of audio gear, the box painted the same dull beige as the ceiling. He reached in, located the breaker labeled MAIN ROOM, and yanked it with a practiced flick of his wrist. The club immediately went dark, all the neon and strobe lights swallowed by a silence so sudden it was almost sacred.

In the blackness, the only light came from the two EXIT signs.

For a heartbeat, nobody moved. Then the crowd began to scream.

The Revenger dropped to his knees, pressed his fists against the grating, and let the shadows come. It was not a power—more like a curse, born from trauma and whatever damage had rewired his nervous system. He could feel the familiar darkness rising, flowing across the floor in slow, sticky waves. He guided it not with thoughts but with feelings, extending a tendril here, a creeping veil there.

The first bouncer came up the stairs, flashlight in hand. The Revenger waited until he was three steps up, then let the darkness flow over the rail and envelop the man's legs. The bouncer fell, his head bouncing off the metal rung, and the Revenger was on him before he could scream. He jabbed his thumb into the man's larynx, crushed the cartilage, and rolled the body out of sight.

The next bouncer was smarter, calling for backup. The Revenger let him live long enough for two more to arrive, then released the shadows again, trapping all three in a cocoon of pressure and silence.

On the dance floor, panic spread outward as bodies rushed toward the exits. The Revenger tracked the wave of chaos, then leapt off the catwalk, landing on a table with enough force to crack the wood and send glasses shattering in all directions.

For a moment, the fleeing crowd stared at him, eyes wide and white in the dim light. He pushed past them, moving with precise efficiency—a left hook to a jaw here, an elbow to the solar plexus there—knocking down obstacles with just enough force.

He was halfway to the VIP lounge before the first flashlight beam found him. He ducked low, rolled under a velvet rope, and burst through the curtain into Vale's sanctum.

The office was a cathedral of decadence. A cherry-red desk, lacquered to a mirror finish, dominated the center of the room. On it sat a pyramid of rolled twenties, a scattering of plastic wristbands, fake IDs, and a large glass ashtray—somehow spotless.

Behind the desk, Vale leaned back in a black leather chair, one leg crossed over the other, wearing a white suit with a silk shirt unbuttoned to the navel. His hair was a neatly styled coif dyed an unnatural shade of yellow.

Even as the Revenger moved toward him, Vale seemed unshaken.

"I know you, don't I?" he said calmly.

The Revenger pounced, landing on the desk, grabbing Vale by the throat, and pulling his face close to his own. The Revenger was all fiend, but Vale only smiled.

"Yes, I do know you. They said you were dead."

The Revenger paused, momentarily confused.

It was long enough for Vale to smash a whiskey bottle over the Revenger's skull, but the impact left no damage. The Revenger didn't even flinch. Now, Vale was afraid.

"Well..." the Revenger answered. "I guess I got better."

Club security quickened their pace toward the office when they heard Vale's shriek. By the time they entered, the Revenger was gone.

Vale was nailed to the desk, mouth agape, with several of the Revenger's daggers embedded in his body.

The Revenger was already behind the wheel of his 1971 Stutz Blackhawk, quietly driving just below the speed limit. A masterpiece of design and power, the car acted as both steed and sanctuary. Its glossy black exterior reflected city lights like liquid night, while the rumbling engine signaled a predator on the hunt. Inside, mahogany and leather evoked elegance, hiding secret compartments for weapons and gear.

Elsewhere, in a confession booth still faintly smelling of last Sunday's incense, Father Elias waited for the next soul in need of absolution. He would eventually learn what had happened in the club and who was responsible. The city was a closed circuit, and ultimately, all currents led back to him.

But for now, there was only the silence of the empty nave and the slow drip of candlewax on the tile. He recited his prayers and waited for the world to need him again.

4

THERE'S NO REDEEMING

The Financial District was a graveyard after dark—thirty blocks of shuttered ambition and double-locked doors. Among the moving things were rats, the pneumatic hiss of distant subway brakes, and the endless, unblinking ticker tapes that lined the facades in sickly orange. And, of course, the Revenger.

The Morgan & Hays Building's lobby was all marble and gold, the kind of showy design meant to distract you from the fact that the men upstairs moved nothing real. Inside, the security guard's desk was empty except for an open copy of a men's magazine and a warm can of Tab. The Revenger scanned the monitors—a wall of CRTs stacked four high and six across. All but three were static, lines of interference ghosting across the grayscale feed. On the remaining screens, he watched the janitorial crew vacuum the twelfth floor, a man in a blue jumpsuit squeegee the front windows, and a woman in a knee-length skirt and white Keds hurry across the lobby clutching a Filofax.

The Revenger stepped past the empty guard booth; his coat brushing the edge of the desk and followed the directory toward the elevators. He pressed the call button. The doors opened immediately—another security failure, or maybe fate. He stepped in, riding the elevator up past countless floors of silent, vacant cubicles, each a microcosm of 1980s gloom: plastic ferns, framed quotes from Sun Tzu.

The fortieth floor spat him out into a literal hall of mirrors, where every surface reflected every movement and flaw, creating a hall of ego polished to a blinding shine.

The office he wanted was at the far end, past the glassed-in bullpen where the high priests of capital made their sacrifices. He walked, boots whispering against the Persian runner, and counted the cameras mounted above every third door.

The target tonight was Vincent O'Donnell, a portfolio manager who had used insider trading and a talent for money laundering to secure a penthouse view and a heart that beat four times faster than normal. The Revenger had watched him at Euphoria more than once, shoveling sushi with one hand and snorting white powder with the other.

Vincent's personal office was a shrine to gluttony: a glass-top desk with a mountain of stacked papers, each commemorating a hostile takeover or a ruined pension fund. And at the center, Vincent O'Donnell, heavyset and hairy, shirtless in his office chair, suspenders hanging at his waist, face powdered with cocaine and sweat.

"Listen, Don, just get the yen before the damn bell, okay? Tell Tokyo we'll double the buy if—" He stopped midsentence.

O'Donnell set the phone down, eyes tracking the silhouette in the doorway.

"How'd you get in here? Nobody's allowed up here right now."

The Revenger said nothing. As he moved, the shadows in the office followed, pooling around his boots. Walking slowly, he swept his arm across the TV bank.

Every screen went black. The only light now was the ticker outside, running in garish orange and reflected a hundred times across the office glass.

"How the hell did you do that?!" O'Donnell grunted.

As the Revenger advanced, O'Donnell began to shout.

"Speak to me! Speak!"

The darkness in the room bled up the walls, warping the angles, swallowing the sharp corners. O'Donnell watched, and his mind for negotiation kicked in. He laid out a few lines of coke on a small mirror and offered it up to the Revenger.

"You want some? Whatever it is, we can work it out. The people I work for can be very forgiving. I mean, we could use someone like you in our employ."

As he spoke, one hand outstretched with the mirror, his other quietly reached for the sawed-off double-barreled shotgun hidden under his desk.

BOOM! A single shot rang out, blowing the Revenger back to the doorway.

"Ha! I got you! I got you now!" O'Donnell bellowed, standing and affixing his suspenders over his bare torso. He smiled, holding the shotgun.

As he walked toward the Revenger, who lay on the office floor, he taunted, "You did Vale, right? Well, you aren't so tough now, are you?"

He stood over the Revenger, searching for a face in the shadows.

"We own this city, pal," he said, loading the shotgun and leveling it at the Revenger's head. "The Baron said to tell you he'll see you in hell."

Inky tendrils of shadow snaked around O'Donnell's ankles and pulled him to the floor. As he lay on his back, stunned, the shadows pinned him like a man about to be drawn and quartered. His big-shot bravado quickly disappeared.

The Revenger shot up from the floor and climbed atop O'Donnell.

"You are a parasite. A ravenous leech. You consume everything around you," the Revenger said with barely a hint of indignation. These were merely facts to him. He pulled the shotgun's spent shells from his stomach, as if the shadows held them aloft.

"Let's see how big your appetite really is," he said, shoving the shells into O'Donnell's open mouth with violent force. The shadows stretched outward from the Revenger, grabbing objects from around the room—a vial of blow, rolls of cash, corrupt paperwork, paperweights, scotch tape, a stapler, several pens, anything they could grasp.

One by one, the shadows shoved more things down O'Donnell's throat.

O'Donnell's eyes widened as he choked. Then his throat exploded open.

Later, at the newspaper, Eleanor's bullpen was a place where time moved in fits and starts, and the only real light came from the blue glow of an IBM Selectric's ready lamp and the washed-out stripe of a fluorescent tube that never stopped buzzing.

She sat buried in a sea of paperwork, elbows deep in the uneven heap of manila folders, autopsy reports, and dog-eared homicide logs. Someone had left a half-eaten bear claw on her desk corner. Beside it was a pyramid of Styrofoam cups, each with a lipstick mark. The coffee tasted like mud, but it kept her from blinking too long.

The newest file was marked "Vincent O'Donnell."

She recognized the name: another of the Baron's secret capos.

This murder was elaborate and deliberately left for someone to discover.

Maybe her.

Whoever you are, she thought, you're just getting started, aren't you?

"I'm going to need more caffeine," she said aloud.

Delgado worked the bodega register and the cigarette rack with a magician's dexterity, ringing up customers while barely looking up. He whistled along with the radio—"Hungry Like the Wolf," volume set low so as not to startle his late-night customers. When he caught his reflection, he looked older than he remembered. Tired.

He saw Eleanor before she opened the door. She moved like a sleepwalker with a mission: hair in a wild knot, trench coat cinched tight against the rain.

She headed straight for the fridge, grabbed a six-pack of Coke, and set it on the counter. Delgado rang her up without comment.

After she left, Delgado locked up, turned the radio to the late-night talk station, and did his rounds of the store. He reached under the counter and took out a package wrapped in brown butcher paper. Inside were six of the throwing knives favored by the Revenger. He put the package in a plastic bodega bag, carried it to the alley behind the shop, and left it by the trash chute.

He lit a cigarette, letting the smoke cut through the chemical smell of the city, and watched the fog swallow the buildings, the sidewalk, the world.

He looked at the empty street and said softly: "Stay sharp, shadow man."

He kept smoking as he began his walk home.

5

JUSTICE SERVED TO EVERYONE

The ironwork surrounding Judge Carlisle's house was both barbed and decorative. The large fence was lined with pointy spikes. The Revenger landed in the gravel border just beyond it, coat tails flaring out and settling into a ripple that faded as quickly as a shiver.

Driven solely by greed, Carlisle had manipulated the law to benefit the Syndicate, keeping the Baron and his followers safe from prosecution. With his grayed sides, bald head, and stiff demeanor, he resembled a caricature of modern aristocracy.

The Revenger crossed the courtyard and dropped into a low crawl, sliding across the narrow patch of grass toward the garage bay. A security guard paced the concrete in a cheap windbreaker, carrying a sidearm that had never been fired. The guard's steps fell into a steady, looping pattern, and the Revenger timed his movements accordingly.

He slipped undetected past the guard and into the main corridor of the judge's home. The house was a shrine to Carlisle himself: wall after wall of civic medals, glass cabinets filled with plaques.

The judge was nearly asleep on a couch in his study, in his bathrobe and slippers, when the Revenger opened the door. Carlisle heard the sound a second too late.

The Revenger forced the judge upright, his spine hitting a bookshelf with a thud. The judge opened his mouth, likely to call out, but the Revenger pressed a finger to his lips—slowly and deliberately—and then to Carlisle's.

Carlisle froze, his breath ragged in his chest.

"All that you've amassed—the house, the cars, the tacky artwork, the wine cellar, the mounted animal heads," the Revenger said softly. "Haven't you ever heard that you can't take it with you?"

"You're a corpse," the judge spat. "We killed you!"

The words threw the Revenger off balance, just as similar feelings of recognition had in Vale's office at Club Euphoria. He knew of the Syndicate by reputation and felt deep in his bones that they needed to be punished. Eliminated.

But how did they know him?

The judge wasn't as quick as Vale, but he still noticed the confusion on the Revenger's face and seized the moment with words rather than weapons.

"What's the matter? You seem confused for a ghost."

The Revenger regained his composure.

"There's only one dead man in here," he said calmly.

Supported by the shadows around them, the Revenger lifted the judge into the air like a WWF wrestler from that era, then threw him through the window. The judge landed on the ornate bars of the outside fence, impaled, blood mixing with the rain.

The Revenger poured several bottles of the judge's brandy all over the study and left a trail down the stairs to the ground floor. He dropped a single match and paused to watch the flames flicker their way upstairs. He was already back in the Blackhawk, safely en route to pick up the new daggers from the bodega, before the fire trucks arrived.

As the smoke rose, so did the legend of the Revenger among the children of the night. Down in the arteries beneath Midtown, where the F train tunneled under the throbbing belly of Manhattan, the world belonged to ghosts and street kids like Echo and Rook.

Echo was slender and light-boned, with a tangle of black hair swept to one side and secured with a twist tie. Rook was taller and skinnier, with wrist bones like tent poles beneath his skin. Both teens moved through the station as if they had built it, backpacks scuffed, shoes taped and held together by memories of what brand names once felt like.

Echo led, her boots squeaking on the greasy tile, a can of black Krylon dangling from one hand and a folded subway map stuffed in the other. She picked a spot beneath, a slab of wall already half obliterated by tags, and set her backpack at her feet.

Rook acted as lookout, eyes scanning the corridor, monitoring the station's pulse—three cleaners in orange jumpsuits, two MTA workers with coffee and cigarettes, a Wall Street type hunched over his Walkman. Rook pulled out his own can—red this time, with a nozzle he'd customized for extra spatter—and nodded to Echo.

She popped the Krylon, inhaled the first burst of aerosol, and got to work. The wall was slick with condensation, but the paint adhered, flowing into streaks that quickly formed the shape of a thin man's silhouette with jagged edges and hollow eyes. She worked quickly, layering black on black, until the figure gradually became recognizable.

Rook admired her hand. He stepped forward and added a thin, arterial slash of red: a pocket square. They didn't talk about what it all meant. Everybody on the street knew. It was the city's new ghost left behind, the one the tabloids called "the Revenger," the one that made even the old-school hitters and the ex-cops shudder.

Rook grabbed Echo's sleeve, and they ducked back toward the tracks, their feet slapping out a rhythm that only made sense to kids who ran everywhere. Echo's heart drummed in her chest. She could hear the trains approaching—the thunder of wheels and the hot wind that always seems to precede them—and for a moment, she felt like the whole city was running with her, every rat and lost soul moving in time.

They reached their hole, a narrow space between the electrical panels and the old signal cabinet. Rook slid the door shut, and they slumped against the wall, breathless and grinning. The station was already beginning to wake, footsteps above echoing down through the pipes and the whine of the third rail.

"Think he'll see it?" Echo asked, wiping sweat from her brow.

Rook shrugged. "I think he always does."

Echo looked down at her hands, paint-flecked and shaking a little from the adrenaline. She wondered if this was what it felt like to be immortal, to leave a mark that nobody could erase.

6

NO RUNNING, NO HIDING, NO ESCAPE

The Revenger parked the Blackhawk beneath an overpass, where rainwater pooled in shivering black lakes along the curb. The car's engine still ticked, cooling its anger. The shadows obeyed as he slipped into an apartment building.

He thumbed the elevator button, watched the cracked plastic spit a spark, and then decided on the stairs. Four flights, no windows, each landing lit by a single forty-watt bulb that sizzled in protest. The banister was sticky, the steps paved with cigarette butts.

On the fifth floor, he found the right door by the color: not the official green that the building super used for touch-ups, but a sludgy brown with paint bubbles. He waited and pictured the layout—a mattress on the floor, a hot plate, a bathroom.

He flexed his hands, letting the shadow gather around his fingers. It wasn't exactly a power—more like a symbiote he'd learned to live with, a darkness that responded when he called. He reached for the knob, and the hallway light dimmed away. The lock was hollow, so the whole jamb caved in, sending splinters across the linoleum.

The target, Warren Pike, was exactly as expected: sprawled on a dirty mattress, eyes half-closed, with a rubber tourniquet still looped around one bicep. He wore only boxers and a stained undershirt, his legs very thin, marked by the blue patterns of old veins. The room was a museum of failure, full of empty beer cans and bent spoons.

Pike had once been a coroner, forging autopsy reports for the Syndicate in exchange for cash and heroin, until his inner demons caused his daily life to grind to a halt. His mind dulled, he rarely stood unless necessary, lying motionless for hours in a dazed haze.

Pike's head lazily moved up, his mouth moving in slow-motion protest, but the Revenger was already across the room. He clamped a hand over the man's face—his palm nearly swallowed the entire jaw—and pinned him back to the mattress. The other hand found the tourniquet, ripped it loose, then used it to bind Pike's wrists.

"Don't," Pike moaned, his voice trembling. "Please. I can talk; I can—"

The Revenger yanked him up by the tied wrists and flung him, shoulder first, through the bathroom door. The tub was already three inches full, its surface cloudy. Old needles floated like reeds, gently bobbing in the sludge. The stench was foul—rotted flesh, old bleach, and a deathly odor that clung to the tiles and walls.

The king of spent laziness in all but name hit the floor, his chin splitting open on the ceramic. The Revenger grabbed him by the hair and forced his face toward the tub.

He held Pike's head beneath the water, hands flat against the man's skull. The junkie kicked, legs thrashing, heels pounding against the side of the tub. For a moment, the surface stayed calm, just a faint swirl of shadow around the submerged face. Then the bubbles appeared: first slow, then frantic. Pike's entire body jerked, knees hitting tile, toes scraping for support. The bathwater froth grew and turned pink at the edges.

He left Pike's body in the filthy tub and made his exit just as quickly as he had arrived. The Blackhawk's engine roared, a war cry thrown into the dark, harsh night.

By the time Eleanor arrived, the city had already tried to swallow the crime.

The precinct had sent uniforms and a forensics van, and together they managed to trample most of the evidence and turn the fifth floor into a holding pen for chain-smoking and bored EMS workers. She walked around the room, her eyes scanning the details. A junkie's hoard: burned-out Bic lighters, takeout boxes.

She spent the next few minutes in the bathroom, taking in the horrifying scene. Then she stepped into the hall for air, letting the memory of the bathroom fade for a moment.

She heard movement on the stairs. A shuffle, almost too soft to notice.

She sensed a shadow moving where the hallway lights didn't quite reach. She followed carefully, every step measured. The shadow turned down the stairwell and disappeared. She paused, the city's noise ringing in her ears, and wondered—not for the first time—if this encounter with the killer was just her imagination.

The skeletal limbs of fire escapes bracketed the alley behind the building. Eleanor moved through it without hesitation, her boots splashing in shallow puddles, the gun in her purse a familiar and comforting pressure. She reached the mouth of the alley and paused, letting her eyes adjust to the low light. The ambient glow from the street bled only as far as the first dumpster, then surrendered to the dark.

She took one step forward, then another, feeling the way the darkness flexed in front of her. It was not empty; the shadow had a thickness, a presence that pulsed in time with her heartbeat. She waited, senses wide open, and in the span of three measured breaths, the Revenger stepped out from the deepest black.

Eleanor gripped the rain-slick wall with her left hand and her concealed weapon with her right. She didn't flinch. "You're working through a list, aren't you?"

The Revenger stood completely still. The only motion was a slow tap of his glove against his thigh—a dull, repetitive click that sounded almost bored. She let the silence spool out between them, then nodded at the car parked just past the mouth of the alley.

"Nice car. Really sells the whole mysterious avenger bit."

He angled his head. "You followed me," he said.

She kept going, undeterred. "Stutz Blackhawk? There aren't many of those roaming the streets at night. Fewer with the custom job." She tried to smile, but her lips were numb from the cold. "You plan on adding me to the list, or am I an asterisk?"

He radiated a resolve that made the alley feel smaller, more private.

She stepped closer, boots squelching in the puddles, until they were three feet apart. "You only hurt people who hurt others. You're dismantling the Syndicate."

She fished a pack of cigarettes from her purse and offered him one.

He tilted his head again. They stood like that for a long moment, the silence interrupted only by the tick of the engine cooling behind them and the slow drip of water off the fire escape. The air between them hummed with possibility—two people perhaps chasing the same goal. She finally lit a cigarette of her own.

"Suit yourself," she said, putting the pack back in her purse.

He moved to the car, opened the door, and slid behind the wheel. She noticed how the shadows swirled and danced around him, like sentient companions.

"What are you?" she asked.

He paused before closing the car door.

"I don't know what I am."

The engine caught, a deep-throated growl that vibrated the puddles into rings.

She watched him drive away, the Stutz Blackhawk's taillights like twin rubies in the wet, before they disappeared behind the next wave of rain and the turn at the end of the block.

7

TORN AND BROKEN

The Revenger had been shadowing the Syndicate courier since the moment the kid left the Meat Market on Gansevoort, all the way to the hole-in-the-wall Italian spot where he traded his envelope for a rolling duffel. The courier was small-time, a runner with more nerves than brains. But the package was said to be a message from the Baron—something to signal to his enemies that, despite the Revenger, it was all business as usual.

As he followed the kid into an alley, something shifted. The air grew thicker. The Revenger let his hand slide inside his coat, fingers brushing the grip of one of his pistols.

Then he saw him. A figure materialized in the negative space between two dumpsters. White on white clothes, no skin visible, and a coat—floor-length, tailored. The figure wore a mask: a smooth, burnished surface that caught no light and gave back no shape. The eyes were lost behind smoked glass, or maybe there were no eyes at all.

The Whisper. The Syndicate's sinister assassin.

The Revenger curled his right hand and let the shadow do its work—oily filaments slid from between his knuckles, pooling around his fist and snaking up his forearm. The Whisper moved like a mirror image of the Revenger, a foul mimicry.

Seemingly unafraid of the shadowy tendrils, the Whisper spoke.

"The Baron sends his regards."

The Revenger glanced toward the courier. The duffel bounced on the curb. He clocked the kid's trajectory, then returned his focus to the threat in front of him. The rain around the Whisper seemed to hesitate, suspended.

A blade appeared in each hand, drawn from somewhere inside the Whisper's coat—a twin set, black steel, the edges almost vibrating with sharpness.

The Revenger drew both pistols.

"Don't you know not to bring a knife to a gunfight?"

The Whisper moved first—a flicker in the periphery—left blade slicing at an oblique, a movement so fine the air itself parted before the steel. The Revenger's right arm snapped up, shadow thickening into a crude shield, and the knife's edge hit it with a wet slap. Shadow bled black mist, grazing the coat and drawing a stinging arm wound.

The Revenger couldn't remember the last time he'd felt physical pain. There was something otherworldly about the Whisper's knives. They seemed to glow, even.

No matter. The Revenger fired both guns at his foe.

Impossibly, the bullets stopped, hovered, and dropped at the Whisper's feet.

The Whisper retreated, pivoting off the balls of his feet, and in a smooth movement planted the heel of his boot into the lid of a trash bin. The trash can tipped over, scattering a flood of glass bottles, soup cans, and the remnants of a dozen slaughterhouse lunches. The debris clattered and bounced across the pavement; the Revenger skated through it, but the Whisper used the chaos to vanish.

The Revenger holstered his pistols and considered the fiend's escape.

Why give up the advantage? Was the Whisper only testing his power?

The answer arrived in a spinning kick that toppled the Revenger. Pain burst hot; he dropped to one knee, and the shadows flickered, losing their shape. The Whisper pressed forward, twin blades a blur. One gouged the Revenger's forearm, slicing through coat and skin. The other aimed for his throat but missed.

He rolled left, kicking the Whisper in the knee with a heel strike that was all hate and no finesse. The assassin's leg buckled, and the Revenger surged up, driving his own knife into the man's ribs. Something gave—a wet, fibrous crunch—and the Whisper hissed: the first sign of pain coaxed from him. One of his knives fell to the ground.

The Revenger followed up with a right hook, shadow-wrapped fist caving in the side of the mask, and then they were both on their feet again, staggering, wet, leaving streaks of red and black across the alley walls.

The Whisper pretended to strike high with his remaining blade, then ducked and punched the Revenger in the gut. The Revenger lashed out with his shadow arm, slamming the Whisper into the brick hard enough to crack mortar and send a shower of brick dust down his coat. He pressed the advantage, pounding fist after fist into the assassin's midsection, feeling the resistance shift from iron to rubber to wet sand.

He seized the assassin's wrist and twisted, snapping the radius with a crisp pop. The second blade fell to the ground, robbing the Whisper of his supernatural advantage. The Whisper smashed his masked head into the Revenger's nose. They both tumbled to the ground. The Revenger rolled—and the Whisper was gone.

Cautiously, he left the alley.

He watched the alley behind him, half expecting the Whisper to return, and wondered if this was what it felt like to be prey. He didn't like it.

But he liked the pain. It made him feel alive.

He found the courier's duffel still sitting by the curb. The kid was long gone.

The bag turned out to be empty.

The fight had been the real message from the Baron. The rules had changed. Now there was an enemy who could match him, move for move, and even hurt him.

8

NO HOLY GHOST FOR THE DEVOUT

Mick "Knuckles" Varnum, the Syndicate's second-in-command when it came to bone-breaking, wasn't large, at least not in the way movies portrayed his type. He was small and stocky, but broad-chested and thick around the neck. His fists were like hammers, and his eyes were close-set enough to give him a perpetual look of dumb rage.

He was the kind of guy who believed the world owed him a living. His desire for vengeance matched the Revenger's, but his motives were cruel. He sought compensation for the smallest imagined slights, unlike the Revenger's code of justice. Bizarrely, Varnum thought of himself as a good Catholic boy. He found his strength "miraculous."

He was the only patron left inside Rosey's Bar, a tiny dive spot whose regulars were all the lawless type. As Rosey poured his shots, he complained they weren't full enough. She finally slammed the whole bottle of cheap whiskey in front of him.

"Here. Pour them yourself, tough guy."

She gruffly excused herself to the restroom, leaving Knuckles alone.

Knuckles felt the Revenger's shadow darken Rosey's doorway.

"You know what I like about you, pal?" Varnum asked, pouring himself another shot without looking in the Revenger's direction. "I get to kill you twice."

This time, the Revenger didn't let the words slow him down. Whatever memories he had lost, whatever secrets the Syndicate kept about his past, the mission came first.

His shadows stretched across the tiny bar, covering Knuckles in black.

"Yeah, yeah, I know, you're magical or something now," Knuckles shrugged. "I've heard. But ain't nobody I can't kill. I've got the power of God himself 'round here."

As Knuckles stood, Rosey emerged from the bathroom. Quickly assessing the impending situation, she returned inside and locked the bathroom door behind her.

The Revenger smiled. "God? God called in sick today."

That was all it took. Varnum came in low, the right fist swinging in a perfect arc at the Revenger's ribs. He ducked, but not enough—the blow landed, the sneaky brass knuckles connecting but doing no harm. The Revenger countered with a palm to the face, catching the bridge of the nose and jamming it back toward the brain.

Varnum grunted, tasted blood, then smiled wider, teeth red and shining. He swung again, this time a left, but the Revenger rode the punch, using the force to pivot and slam his shoulder into Varnum's gut, driving them both into Rosey's old jukebox.

Varnum wrapped his arms around the Revenger's midsection and squeezed, trying to crush him into compliance. Shadows, like extra arms, broke Varnum's grip.

Knuckles put up both fists, the brass on each flashing momentarily. Under the brass, jailhouse ink on one hand read "HOLY" across the knuckles. The other said "GOST."

Varnum was many things, and smart wasn't one of them.

The shadows now cloaked the entire bar in darkness. Confused, Knuckles swung wildly without connecting a single time. He switched tactics, shooting in at the Revenger's legs like a wrestler, but the shadows responded, wrapping one of Varnum's forearms and snapping it back in a clean, efficient motion. Varnum howled.

"It's not possible," he said in disbelief. "I'm the wrath of God! Not you!"

Varnum knelt. The Revenger slowly pulled out two of his new daggers.

"Your theology, it seems," he said, raising one dagger high, "is misguided."

The Revenger drove the knives into Varnum's neck, killing him.

As he left Rosey's Bar, the Revenger felt eyes on him from a nearby rooftop. Two kids—Echo and Rook. They knew the names, had seen their tags all over the city: Revenger silhouettes splashed with red. They were mini legends themselves, artists slipping through cracks and coming out the other side grinning. Echo's hair looked white tonight, or at least in the city's poor light. Rook was all angles and shadow, holding a spray can in one hand and a pack of smokes in the other. They leaned out over the edge, eyes wide, jaws dropped, as if they'd just seen the second coming.

They watched as the Revenger drove away in what was the coolest car they'd ever seen in real life. When he was gone, they scrambled down the fire escape. Echo ran into Rosey's, to the spot where Varnum still sprawled, and crouched down, watching the blood flow, watching the way the man's hand twitched and then, finally, went still.

Rosey emerged from the back and shouted, "Get out of here, you little rats!"

Echo and Rook disappeared into the night.

9

SEE YOUR DEMISE

It had been roughly a week since the Revenger took out the low-level traffickers in the subway, with each night delivering a new moment of justice. From a roof under a water tower, he fixed his gaze on the second floor of an old factory. A latticework of broken windows, the glass jagged and frosting over with cold, gave way to the glow of half a dozen cigarettes and the blue pulse of a flickering fluorescent.

This was where Victor Kaine, one of the Baron's remaining captains, quietly gathered a small group of Syndicate thugs whose trust in leadership had grown shaky. Victor always, in secret, imagined himself the Baron's better, waiting for the right moment to ascend by any means necessary. The so-called Revenger now provided him with a lucky opportunity.

Machiavellian in his scheming, Kaine finally planned to take command.

Four men and two women sat at the table, with Kaine at its head. He gestured as he spoke, each sweep of his wrist punctuated by a little cloud of smoke.

The Revenger closed his eyes and felt for the shadow. Even out here, with the night so thin and the city's light pressing in, he could summon it. A current of cold ran up his arms, pooling at his fingertips. He let it go, watched as the shadow slipped across the brick face of the building, up and over the broken glass, seeping through the cracks in the window frames until it hovered, weightless, just behind Victor's head.

Inside, the conspirators sat clustered around a battered conference table, their coats still on, hunched against the cold. A yellowed blueprint of the Lower West Side was pinned to the wall, thumbtacks outlining delivery routes and dead-drop points in the grid of city blocks. The air in the room was a mixture of nicotine and sweat, so thick that the exposed pipes overhead dripped black with condensation.

Victor raised his voice, the tail end of a joke arcing into a threat. "I'm telling you, the Baron's gone soft. He thinks this city's still afraid of him? Captains drop like flies!"

The man to Victor's right—tall, blond, twitchy—leaned in. "So, what's the play?"

Victor snapped his lighter shut then let it clatter across the tabletop. "Shipment hits Pier 17 at midnight, just like always. Only this time, we're not handing it off to the Baron's boys. We cut the feed, lock the place down, and when he shows up for his taste, we put him down like a sick dog."

He splayed his hands, as if presenting an offering to the table. "We run the district. We name the price. The rest of the Syndicate falls in line—or they fall, period."

One of the others—a younger kid with a pencil mustache and a fresh shiner under his eye—sucked air through his teeth. "You sure about this, Kaine? Last guy who tried to gossip about the Baron like this, they found his tongue nailed to his own front door."

Victor smiled, sharp as a blade. "Do I look scared?"

The Revenger drifted the shadow closer, letting the edges bleed over the faces at the table. He heard every word, every shift of feet, every clink of glass.

The tall one cracked his knuckles, eyes darting to the window. "Even if we pull this off, there's still him. The Revenger. You really think he'll just let it go?"

Victor's smile twitched. "He's just a myth. A ghost story for guys too old to believe in the boogeyman. You know what gets rid of a ghost?" He flicked the ash from his cigarette, letting it drift to the filthy floor. "You turn on the lights."

The Revenger drew the shadow tight around his fingers, then sent a thin tendril slipping through the tiniest crack in the window frame. The temperature in the room dropped by a degree, maybe two. Enough for the men at the table to notice, for one of them to shiver and rub at his neck like he'd just been breathed on.

Victor's eyes narrowed. "Are you cold, Riley?"

The man called Riley—short, broad shoulders, ex-cop by the look of him—

swallowed and forced a laugh. "Just the draft. This place gives me the creeps."

Victor sneered. "Get a grip. We're making history here."

The shadow curled around Riley's throat. Not choking, just a gentle squeeze. He gasped, eyes wide. Riley slumped lower in his seat, silence replacing whatever protest he might have offered. It appeared he'd simply nodded off.

Victor stood, the new king of nothing, and basked in the attention of his new team. The Revenger let the tendril of shadow retract, then faded back from the window.

He mentally mapped the exits, the angles. Every detail. Victor had posted two men at the north and south doors, another two on the catwalks. The last, a beanpole with hollow cheeks and a jitter that made him shake out his hands every few seconds, kept to the perimeter, circling with a sawed-off tucked under his coat.

Headlights sliced through the fog as the Baron's black Mercedes drew near. Victor wasn't expecting this surprise. The Baron was onto his attempted coup.

Four bodyguards exited and positioned themselves around the car, solid and confident. The Baron himself appeared last, embodying the image of an old-money assassin—early sixties, muscular, thinning hair slicked back, walking slowly as if daring anyone to stop him.

Victor scrambled to the door and nervously greeted the boss. "Baron! We weren't expecting you here. Come in!" The Baron looked him over, then raised a single finger. His men drew pistols and shot almost everyone at Victor's table. Even Riley, who, unbeknownst to them, was already dead.

Only the man with the pencil-thin mustache remained. The Baron fixed his gaze upon his would-be successor as the mustache man crept up behind Victor.

Victor felt the knife at his throat before the man spoke.

"I tried to tell you, Vic, what happens to those who cross the Baron."

Suddenly, the shadows of the Revenger killed all the light.

Muzzle flashes stuttered in the dark, blind and desperate.

The Revenger had drifted from his perch into the factory's rafters. He let the shadow pulse in his hands, thin tendrils creeping along the floor. He sent it under boots, up trouser legs, into collars—everywhere the nerves were raw and closest to the skin. He let the cold seep in, just enough to make the shooters believe in ghosts, just enough to get them questioning what they were really shooting at.

The Revenger split the shadow, sent a piece of it curling into Victor's ear.

"They're turning on you," he whispered, modulating the voice until it matched the one Victor had used to mock Riley. "They think you're weak."

Victor spun, pistol raised, and shot into nothingness.

The Revenger maintained the pressure. He whispered to one of the guards—"They're behind you"—and the man turned, firing into the darkness with a scatter of bullets that hit the Baron's man on the inside, the one with the thin mustache. Victor's guards had stormed in and were slaughtered by accidental friendly fire.

The confusion lasted all of thirty seconds, during which the Baron quietly escaped. Everyone else was dead except for Victor, who crawled toward the nearest exit, blood pouring from his side. He sensed the Revenger was near and crawled behind a crate instead, putting pressure on his wound and reloading his gun. He muttered to himself, a litany of old-school curses and self-reassurances.

"Not real," he hissed. "This is the really real world. This can't be happening!"

Ever the slick negotiator, he yelled into the black. "Hey, Revenger! You want to take down the Syndicate? I can help you…"

He finished reloading, already planning his next double-cross.

The shadows caught Victor's gun hand and squeezed, winding around his wrist and elbow, leeching the strength until the gun clattered to the floor.

"What is this power?" Victor screamed. "It should be mine! Not a dead man's! Everything should have been mine! The Syndicate! The power! The fear! The city!"

The Revenger spoke. "You know, you all keep saying I'm dead."

Victor laughed, a panicked rasp. "That's right! You were dead!"

The Revenger drew his pistols.

"Who knows? Maybe you can come back, too?"

BLAM. BLAM.

"Though I doubt it."

Elsewhere, the Tribune newsroom pulsed with a rhythm all its own—the antiphonal slam of typewriter keys, the high-lonesome ring of three desk phones at once, the ozone of burnt coffee and just-past-legal nicotine. Eleanor sat at her cubicle, shoulders squared, hunched over the half-finished draft that would either make her city's next obsession or get her canned.

Frank Donovan, her editor, hovered at her elbow, blue Oxford rumpled, tie askew.

"You can't use 'Revenger' in the headline," he said, voice pitched low, eyes flicking to the chaos of the bullpen as if someone might overhear the future and steal it. "You want the city to take this guy seriously? You call him what he is: a murderer."

She spun in her chair and fixed him with a stare. "You want me to run with 'Mysterious Vigilante Stalks Syndicate'? Fine. But the street already has a better name for him."

Frank exhaled and ran a palm over his jaw, fingers digging into three days of stubble. "Fine. 'The Revenger.' But don't you make him a folk hero."

She raised both hands in mock salute. "Scout's honor."

As dawn broke, the Revenger stood across from a newsstand.

He watched as the first delivery trucks arrived, groaning to a stop, back doors swinging open to unload the day's newspapers by the hundred. Bundles of Tribune thudded onto the pavement. The vendor, a stocky guy wearing a Yankees cap, sliced the strings with a box cutter and began stacking papers under the scarred plastic window.

The Revenger leaned in, listening to the rhythm of the street. It was the same everywhere: disbelief, then fascination, then the slow creep of hope.

Delgado's bodega opened earlier than usual. He shuffled outside to smoke a cigarillo and read the headlines. He glanced at the alley, squinting, and spotted the Revenger. Delgado nodded, a subtle tilt of his chin. The Revenger gently nodded back.

Echo and Rook, the two kids from the tunnels, perched on the fire escape above the bodega with their legs dangling over the edge. Rook saw him first, smiled, and held up a stolen Tribune, front page visible. Echo pretended to bow, then flipped him the bird. They scrambled back inside, their voices echoing through the iron ribs of the building.

10

ALL TRUE EVIL COMES TO THE LIGHT

It was a little before seven, and the Waldorf Astoria's main ballroom was populated with the city's new aristocracy, rubbing elbows with the press and socialites.

Eleanor paused at the threshold. They had draped the hall in white velvet, as if to bleach out the city's rot; the stage at the far end shimmered under a fleet of imported crystal. At the foot of the dais, an ice sculpture—twenty pounds of swan, bleeding into a tray of caviar—presided over a table of hors d'oeuvres.

She saw the social hierarchy without looking: the hedge-funders clustering near the champagne towers, their suits sharp enough to open veins; the politicos—younger, leaner, already hunting for the next hand to shake or back to stab; the TV crews circling the edges, prepping for the eight o'clock live feed. Even the air felt divided, the temperature dropping a degree every twenty feet, as if the walls themselves understood who mattered.

Her press badge itched at her neck. She flicked it out, letting the city's insignia reflect in the glass as she sidestepped a photographer positioning himself for the best angle on the caviar swan. Her hair was up—not for effect but to keep it out of the cocktail sauce—and her coat, thrift-store camel, two sizes too big, made her look like she'd borrowed it from a dead cop. She liked the effect; it kept the campaign hacks at a distance.

Clark Hargrove was the evening's main attraction: over six feet tall, blond, handsome, like a character out of a Bret Easton Ellis novel. He wore a navy single-breasted suit and a smile that was all teeth and no warmth. He had security blended in—two ex-military guys in off-the-rack tuxedos, each with the posture of someone who had killed before. They circled Hargrove as he made his rounds, eyes scanning the edges, never allowing the crowd to distract them.

Councilman Hargrove was long rumored to be a key part of the Syndicate machine, but no law or newspaper had been able to connect him. The evidence was always just out of reach.

She scanned the room for Rook and Echo, kids she knew—expecting them to show up in the periphery as waitstaff or party crashers—but saw nothing. Either they'd found a better gig, or they were waiting for the right moment to be seen.

The lights dimmed. A ripple of anticipation moved through the crowd as the reporters marshaled themselves for the coming spectacle. The stage manager, a thin woman in a headset and sneakers, hustled the anchor and Hargrove toward the dais, where the microphone had been wiped and reset twice in the past ten minutes.

Eleanor slipped closer, positioning herself just off to the side of the podium. The live-feed light blinked amber, then red. The Channel 9 anchor smiled, then turned to Hargrove, who straightened his tie and stared into the void with the hollow conviction of a man who knew what was coming but hoped to outrun it.

She saw, just for a second, a flicker of shadow in the back of the ballroom. Nothing moved, and yet everything did. She gripped the edge of her notepad, waiting.

The Revenger had entered the Waldorf Astoria the way a virus enters a cell: by the dumb, blind luck of a flaw in the perimeter and the certainty of its own intent.

He reached the AV corridor behind the ballroom, where the media machinery thrummed. Server racks and switchboards lined the walls, the air a soup of electromagnetic haze and the ozone of overtaxed transformers.

The control room was a theater of chaos, but a precise one. Five men and one woman in headsets manned the console, their faces lit by the glow of a hundred screens. The director—a guy with hair the color of printer toner—shouted orders over the hum, gesturing with a pencil as if conducting the whole city.

"Ready on Camera Three! Standby, we're bringing up the satellite..."

The Revenger waited in the shadows by the door, watching the rhythm, the tempo, the way the room forgot the world beyond its own walls.

He entered without a word.

The techs were slow to notice, their attention divided among the screens, but when one finally looked up, the Revenger pointed at the exit, shadows billowing.

"Go."

They bolted, a tangle of limbs and confusion, abandoning the board in record time. The Revenger unclipped a folder from his belt and spread it across the console. He sorted the documents: bank statements from a numbered account in the Caymans, transfers matching perfectly with Hargrove's campaign donations. Photos of Hargrove in his clandestine role as Syndicate captain. A separate, sealed envelope contained the real trophy: transcripts and surveillance from a safe house in Astoria linking Hargrove to a vice ring and a chain of police payoffs. The papers inside were stamped with the logo of an internal-affairs task force that, according to every official source, had been disbanded in 1981.

Councilman Hargrove gripped a glass of champagne, face composed but eyes tracing the corners of the room with a reptilian paranoia. He moved to the stage.

The Revenger flicked the sound on, letting the room's ambient noise filter through: a thousand conversations, a hundred clinks of glass, a handful of nervous giggles from the press corps. Somewhere in the background, an elevator dinged, and the ballroom doors yawned open to admit the final wave of guests.

It was almost time.

At exactly eight, the ballroom lights dimmed again. The crowd hushed, the press raised pens and recorders, and the Channel 9 anchor cleared her throat for the camera.

"Good evening, New York," she said, and the city's attention locked in.

Hargrove hit the podium like a televangelist—head high, arms spread to draw in the love of the room, and the crowd leaned forward as if awaiting a sermon.

He began with the usual: "Tonight, we gather not just to celebrate this city but to claim it, ro rescue its soul..." His voice was liquid, every word a syrup poured over the crowd.

"...from the grip of darkness and decay, from those who believe—"

The Revenger began his show.

The ballroom's screens flickered once, then twice. The audio feed cut mid-sentence, replaced by the sizzle and pop of a microcassette queued to the worst moment. On every monitor, every TV, every broadcast tuned to Channel 9, the first document appeared: a bank statement with Hargrove's name in the header, followed by a slow scroll of wire- transfer data, each line a confession in ones and zeros.

Eleanor was first to move. She didn't duck. She raised her notebook, thumbed the tape recorder, and watched the room go feral in under twenty seconds.

Security hit the stage, all hands on Hargrove. The Channel 9 anchor tried to wrap it up, but her voice was lost in the feedback. Half the crowd stood, ready to flee, but the doors were already swarmed by hotel staff, security, and the first guests to realize the event had turned. The AV feed switched again: a slideshow of photos, time-stamped, each more damning than the last. Hargrove with a girl—maybe sixteen, face blank, arm bruised, the background an expensive suite in this very hotel.

The crowd was silent for a few seconds, then the panic began: the sharp intake of breath, the low murmurs, the first shriek from a woman near the front.

From the AV room, the Revenger watched Hargrove's face go slack. The councilman tried to recover, but the feed cut again, and now the room echoed with the warble of a tape, his own voice unmistakeable:

"This is a message from the Baron. The Baron runs this city."

On the monitors, chaos bloomed: security converging on the stage, Hargrove ducking to find the off switch on the podium, the Channel 9 anchor shrieking and diving for cover as if the words might infect her.

The Revenger left the AV room as he'd entered it, a ripple in the building's nervous system.

Hargrove, still onstage, was frozen in the crosshairs of every lens. Behind him, the shadows bled across the wall—not cast by anything visible, but growing, swelling, until they coalesced into the rough outline of a man, taller than Hargrove, with a blur where the face should be. The shadow didn't move at first, but it pulsed, as if waiting for the world to catch up. For a second, the whole room stilled.

The guests, servers, press—all of them, mouths agape.

Hargrove spun around. He saw the shadow, how it moved independently of every light in the room—how it curled around the edges of reality. He staggered, then tried to run, but security caught him, unsure whether to protect him from the crowd or the air itself.

The shadow reached Hargrove. The councilman went limp. The shadow leaned in, and Eleanor, closer than any sane person, heard it whisper in his ear.

"All that pride. The stress will kill you."

Hargrove died without violence. His own heart attacked him.

He collapsed, dead weight in the arms of his own men. The shadow dissolved, not back into the wall but into the thick air behind the dais. The screens flickered, then stayed on Hargrove writhing on the floor as police and medics rushed the stage. It looped, replaying the documents, the photos, the tape.

The ballroom emptied itself, some guests running, some in shock, a few vomiting into potted plants or onto the marble floors. Eleanor was the last to leave. She tucked the notebook under her arm and snapped a Polaroid of the stage.

Outside, the city pulsed with rumor. Already, TVs in bars and bodegas replayed the hack, the legend growing with every retelling. The Waldorf's steps were filled with cops, reporters, and a fresh layer of panic. The city itself felt changed forever.

11

YOU'LL DIE BELIEVING

The church at 8th and Avenue B had once been a Polish parish; now it was a TV studio in disguise. The saints were gone, the niches re-paneled, the altar replaced by a stage with a plexiglass pulpit and a drum kit behind a squealing acrylic shield. A vinyl banner hung where stained glass used to be:

HEALING • PROSPERITY • TONIGHT

Outside, a satellite truck idled, antenna craned like a praying mantis. Inside, a phone bank lined the transept—teen volunteers in headset mics whispering, "Yes, ma'am, we'll take your pledge; press the pound key now."

The Revenger came up the alley, staying in the runoff shade of the eaves.

The nave blazed. Rows of votives were gone; in their place, towers of can lights and two shoulder-mounted Beta cams sweeping the crowd. Every pew was packed. Pastor Daniel Petrokowski stood onstage with a navy suit, gold tie, and his hair sprayed into a helmet. He held a wireless mic like he was born with it. A pristine Bible lay open on the plexiglass.

"In this city," he said, voice thick with faux purpose, "the wicked prosper."

He waited for the applause sign—an actual plywood rectangle above the camera riser—and got it on cue. "But there is a power that will not be mocked."

The Revenger moved the perimeter: past a rack of wet umbrellas, past a merch table stacked with seed-faith envelopes and cassette tapes. Two Syndicate men loitered near the side exit, tuxedos a size too small, lapel mics hissing. Three ushers in polyester blazers worked the aisles with buckets with "GIVE" painted on them.

From a pocket of darkness near the sound booth, the Revenger commanded the shadows. They rose obediently, a slow tide at his boots, then flowed along the baseboards toward the stage, thin as breath.

Petrokowski paced, hand raised, eyes everywhere and nowhere.

"You have seen it—miracles on this very stage." He turned back toward the screen wall, where a blue synth pad leaked from the speakers.

The Revenger exhaled and sent a filament of darkness up the rear wall, across the lighting truss, and onto the projection surface.

Then, an image—high-contrast, hard-edged, like a security feed—of Petrokowski in a back office with his Syndicate handlers counting rubber-banded cash.

The room hiccupped. A few clapped reflexively; a few laughed; most stared.

"The Devil is a liar!" Petrokowski said too fast. "Do not be deceived!"

The Revenger stepped from the dark, letting the light find half his face and refuse the rest. The crowd parted the way a wound opens. Petrokowski's voice climbed.

"These are tricks. Sorcery." He lifted the Bible like a badge.

The Revenger walked to the front row without hurry and stopped at the low step of the stage. The shadow at his feet swelled, and the can lights dimmed.

"You are the sorcerer—a cheap magician. A fraud," he said.

The first Syndicate man lunged. The Revenger let the punch graze, caught the wrist, and turned it until bone gave. The second drew a knife; the Revenger pressed his elbow down and through the pew arm—wood split, bone followed.

Petrokowski tried for the sacristy door—now a greenroom with a powder mirror and a rack of spare suits—but the Revenger vaulted the stage, boots thudding hard enough to shake the mic stands. He caught Petrokowski by the collar and dragged him back beneath the screen.

"It's time to confess your sins," the Revenger said.

The shadows rose, a collar of night around the Syndicate sycophant's throat, lifting him just enough that his polished loafers scraped the scuffed laminate. The camera operator forgot to cut. The live monitor showed the pastor's face flushing from pink to plum, eyes watering, lips trying to form one last sales pitch.

The Revenger lowered him gently, hand at the small of his back like a nurse steadying a patient. He leaned toward Petrokowski's ear.

"Confess," he said again, softer. For a heartbeat, it sounded almost like mercy.

The pastor broke. On live TV, into a mic that carried to countless living rooms and the phone bank beside them, Daniel Petrokowski sobbed and named it all—the cash, the girls, the payoffs, the bodies—each word a nail pulled from a rotten beam.

The remaining congregants began to approach, anger in their hearts.

"Please don't kill me," Petrokowski begged.

"God loves…" the Revenger answered.

"That's right! That's right! God loves!"

The Revenger's eyes scanned the angry mob of scorned believers. He looked back at the preacher and finished the sentence.

"…Man kills."

The Revenger released Petrokowski to the crowd, who fell upon him in a frenzy.

As he left, he knew the people would tear the preacher apart.

12

EVERY WOUND, EVERY SCAR

The Revenger stood at the roof's edge, one foot on the slick ledge, his silhouette outlined by the flickering glow of the neon Zephyr sign across the street.

"VACANCY" was the only word still lit, and even that was false.

The street below was as empty as a drained vein.

The Whisper appeared along the seam of a maintenance hatch, body language an essay in disregard. The white coat hung open, revealing nothing. The mask was different this time, less like a face and more like an unmarked gravestone: seamless, with mirrored lenses that caught the neon and reflected it in shards.

The two men circled, three meters apart, footsteps drowned in the hiss of water rushing down the pitch. The Revenger's coat was darker from the rain, its hem so soaked it clung to the air behind him like a shadow with a mind of its own. His left hand hung by his side, fingers flexing in time with the thunder. His right gripped his knife.

The Whisper spoke first, voice filtered by the mask into something occult.

"Wondering why my knives work on you, when others do not?"

The Revenger grimaced. "I'm wondering why you never shut up."

The Whisper kept moving, coat billowing in the crosswind, never taking the same shape twice. "Look at us. Two sides of the same coin. Sadly, there can be only one."

"Then let's skip the conversation," the Revenger said, stopping by a rusted vent stack, body angled for violence.

The Whisper obliged. He moved suddenly and smoothly, without warning or tension. One second there was space between them, the next it was gone, filled with his body and one of the two knives the Revenger knew could kill him humming toward his throat.

The Revenger ducked, slashing out with his own blade, and felt it connect with the other's rib with a firm, satisfying thump. The Whisper grunted, adjusted, and moved sideways with a blur that was not quite supernatural, but close.

The Revenger feinted low, then brought his knife up in a brutal uppercut. The Whisper caught the blow on his forearm, but not before the tip left a shallow furrow in the pristine white cloth, darkening the sleeve.

This time, the Revenger's slipped under a loose sheet of corrugated tin and rolled to the opposite edge of the roof. The city lights below offered no witness, but he knew at least two pairs of eyes were watching: Echo and Rook, hidden away on a neighboring rooftop, rooting for him.

He let the shadow build at his feet—his trick, his ace, the thing that made him both more and less than human. The rooftop darkened, color draining away until there was nothing but shape and threat.

"Yes, you have power," the Whisper confessed. "But it is power that I can take from you. Before this night is over, you will be truly dead, and I will own the darkness."

He lunged, both knives flashing as he jabbed repeatedly. The Revenger dodged each strike, though not easily, then countered with a left hook that connected with the Whisper's jaw. The mask cracked along the cheek, revealing dark glass and a hint of flesh. The Whisper staggered, but it was a feint. He spun, slashing with the knives, and caught the Revenger's coat, opening a gash along the ribcage that burned like acid.

The Revenger stepped back, trying to gauge the blood flow.

The Whisper circled.

The Revenger let the shadows expand, tentacles of it unfurling from the hem of his coat, wrapping his knife, his arms, his legs, until he was less a man than a weaponized shape. The Whisper hesitated. Just a flicker, but that was all it took. The Revenger leaped, shadow trailing him, and drove his knife at the Whisper's knife hand.

The blade clattered to the rooftop, skipped twice before vanishing over the edge to the alley below. For one glorious second, the Revenger was on top, straddling his enemy, knife at the throat, shadow binding the wrists.

But the Whisper was ready. He twisted, wrenching the shadow-binding tight enough to break his own wrist, and headbutted the Revenger square in the nose. Cartilage popped, blood spurted. The Revenger recoiled stunned, and the Whisper drove a knee into his side, reopening the gash with precision.

The Whisper, now on top, he plunged his remaining knife into the same gash.

For the first time, maybe ever, the Revenger screamed.

"Can you feel the blade's power as it weakens you, as it absorbs your own, as it brings back a flood of forgotten traumas? The memory of your first death?"

The Whisper's words rang true. The Revenger felt all those things: his strength fading, his forgotten past unspooling in a flood of broken images. His death. His rebirth. All of it overwhelming and confusing him.

Maybe it was over. He hadn't completed his mission, no, but he felt the will to fight disappear with each new twist of the knife.

Then the Whisper screamed.

The Revenger's eyes shot open. He saw Rook on the Whisper's back as Echo sprayed paint into the fiend's open face wound, into the eye exposed by his broken mask.

The Whisper flung Rook from his back and across the roof and dispatched Echo with a swift kick to the chest. Rook slid to the edge, his fingertips barely holding him from plunging below to his doom.

The Revenger willed the shadows to pull Rook to safety.

The Whisper staggered. With his remaining dagger, he pointed at the Revenger, the gesture equal parts salute and promise. "Next time, I'll drag your ghost back to hell."

He stepped to the ledge, paused, and with a flourish that mocked gravity, vaulted to the next building, landing hard but upright. He didn't look back.

The Revenger lay bleeding and shivering, neon strobing across his eyes: red and blue and red again. Rook and Echo ran to his side.

Somewhere below, a siren wailed, then died.

The city went back to sleep, oblivious and infinite.

For a few minutes, even the Revenger allowed himself to rest.

13

OUT OF THE DARK I RISE FOR YOU

The rain-drenched streets shimmered beneath the neon lights of Saints and Sinners, an old diner that had seen better days. Inside, the air smelled of fried food and burnt coffee, and the booths hummed with stories and secrets.

Rook and Echo slid into a cracked vinyl booth at the back. Rook looked around. The chimes above the diner door jingled as Father Elias entered, shaking the rain from his coat. The priest's presence drew attention, his eyes sweeping the room before settling on Rook and Echo. He slid into the booth across from them, his expression serious.

"You kids shouldn't be out here alone," he murmured, glancing toward a group of older teens huddled at the counter, voices low and urgent.

"Why? What's happening?" Echo asked, though she knew the answer.

"I think you both already know what's happening," he answered.

Rook's brow furrowed. "We do. And we're not afraid."

"We can handle ourselves, Father," Echo added.

Elias sighed, concern etched deep in his features.

He'd known them since the orphanage, before they fled into the streets and made the pavement their home. He also knew they were tough, resilient, and well-meaning. But he worried about how much they adored the Revenger. He wanted something better for them.

Still, he trusted God to keep watch.

Later that evening, Echo and Rook made their way to Delgado's Bodega, their footsteps splashing the puddles as they navigated the familiar path. The scent of old bread and cleaning solution greeted them as they pushed through the door, the bell chiming softly above.

Delgado stood behind the counter, scanning the street through the security feed. He was a man carved by time and experience—ex-military, with scars etched deep into his skin and shadows behind his eyes that spoke of loss. Rook had heard the whispers: a soldier who had seen too much, who had lost friends in battles, wars that continued in his mind.

"Morning," Delgado said, his voice gravelly but steady. He regarded the two teens with caution and curiosity. "What brings you here?"

"We want to talk to you about him," Echo said, her tone determined.

Delgado leaned against the counter, folding his arms. "I'm not running a fan club in here," he said, his smile betraying the tough talk.

Rook met his gaze. "Then why do you help him?"

Delgado hesitated, memories flooding his mind—the faces of comrades lost in battles fought for reasons now lost to him. "He's fighting a war at home," he said, finally. "One we can't afford to ignore."

As Delgado's words hung in the air. The teens exchanged glances, the gravity of their mission settling over them.

The war. Each side needed its general, and the Baron was top of the food chain for the fiends.

Eleanor had tracked the Baron from a distance, piecing together fragments of information that painted a disturbing picture. Tonight was her chance to uncover the truth.

As she approached the abandoned Mercy General annex, she felt the weight of the building's history pressing down on her. Inside, the air was colder, filled with the metallic tang of long-forgotten horrors. Eleanor crept through the corridors, her heart racing as she recalled tales of experiments gone wrong. She spotted a door marked LAB 3C and paused.

This was the place.

Eleanor pressed her ear against the door, listening for sounds within. She heard the faint hum of machinery, the pulse of something alive. Taking a deep breath, she pushed the door open, revealing a room filled with shadows. The stark white walls glowed under fluorescent lights, There were rows of cages—some held rats, others the grotesque remnants of failed experiments.

Her stomach lurched at the sight, but she steeled herself, focusing on the nearest terminal. She approached, waking it with a tap. The login screen flashed—a default user, admin. As she scrolled through the data, her breath quickened. The logs detailed cell hybridization tests, each marked with a chilling success rate. The implications hit her like a punch to the gut.

A sudden noise echoed from the hallway, footsteps growing closer. Panic surged within her. She shut down the monitor. She held her breath, praying she wouldn't be discovered.

She had to get out. She waited for the footsteps to fade, then bolted toward the exit.

Sliding out the back door into the dark alley, took a moment to breathe.

The Baron's experiments were cruel. Unholy.

He had to be exposed.

14

A DEATH YOU CAN'T SURVIVE

The fortress at 77 West Harrow stood like a sentinel—sixteen stories of stone and glass obscuring the city's light. Rain poured down in sheets, turning the air into a dark haze. Steam hovered over the subway grates, as if it were shrinking back from the height.

A police scanner crackled from a nearby bodega, the voice monotone, reporting midnight stabbings in Queens and stalled ambulances in Midtown, droning like the death knell of a forgotten world.

Under the flickering glow of a streetlamp, the Revenger watched the city pulse with life and decay. Pain throbbed in his side from his last encounter with the Whisper, but the shadows began to stitch him back together, pooling around his boots, ready to obey his call. Each pulse reminded him of the stakes at hand—the lives he had to save, the wrongs he had to right.

He slipped into the building with practiced ease. Ascending floor by floor, each level brought him closer to the heart of the fortress—a heart he intended to stop.

The fourth floor's cubicles had disappeared, with glass partitions covered in peeling paper and replaced by a field hospital for machines. Rows of oscilloscopes and patch bays lined the walls like sentinels left to decay, spools of tape scattered around—relics of a time when this place still mattered. A wall of humming CRTs displayed angles of the tower, their halos fading like dying stars.

On one screen, he glimpsed himself entering the lobby minutes ago.

Suddenly, a wrench whistled through the air and struck a console. Sparks flew, and the sharp smell of burning plastic filled his nostrils. The man wielding it was a Syndicate enforcer—old, heavyset, and surprised by the Revenger's presence.

The Revenger moved instinctively—shoulder into ribs, conduit into kidney. A monitor shattered under the weight of the fight, glass and teeth breaking in unison as the big man crashed into a nest of power cords, the current lighting up his jaw like a flickering neon sign.

With the enforcer down, the Revenger cut the main feed, causing the screens to go black until only his reflection remained, a dark silhouette in the void. He clenched his fists, feeling his resolve grow stronger. This was only the beginning.

The fifth floor split in two: a damp-smelling maintenance hall to the left and a gleaming corridor to the right, where brass kick plates and reinforced glass stood watch. Inside was a rectangle of money, seemingly tidy. Shrink-wrapped bricks sat on pallets; cash floated in sprinkler runoff like drowned butterflies.

Fire doors sealed the room when the halon system activated upstairs.

Three men stood guard, eyes wide and shoes soaked, dressed in rented tuxedos barely concealing their illusions of power. The Revenger stepped into the room, the coldness of it crawling up his spine.

The first tuxedo fired, spraying water through the air instead of aiming directly. The shadow tendrils responded by forcing the man's mouth open and suffocating him. The second lunged with a knife, but the Revenger disarmed him with a quick twist, leaving the attacker gasping. The third tried to run behind a wheeled safe, but the Revenger drew his pistol and fired precisely to eliminate the last threat.

The metal groaned as a pressure door began to lower—a barrier designed to seal a breach. He had only seconds. Grabbing a pallet jack, he pushed it against the door at shin height.

As he continued up the tower, he felt the weight of purpose pressing against him. The Baron awaited at the top.

On the ninth floor, the corridor opened into a stark room: gurneys chained to eyelets in the walls, IV stands toppled, a stainless-steel sink stained with blood.

A half dozen men stepped out quietly, their skin waxy and eyes rimmed yellow, wielding tools that weren't guns—a chain, a crowbar, a hammer, and a surgical saw with a frayed cord. Each wore a hospital gown, reminders of the failed experiments.

Without hesitation, he moved to confront them. The chain swung low; he sidestepped, kicking swiftly to send the man sprawling and scattering teeth across the floor. The crowbar came down, but he deflected it and responded with a brutal punch that left the attacker gasping.

The hammer swung wide, and the Revenger pivoted, taking out the next man with a single gunshot. The saw clattered to the tile as the last two backed away, realizing they had stepped into a nightmare they couldn't comprehend. Those still breathing soon weren't—each marked by a throwing knife buried in the neck.

Finally, the office penthouse at the top.

The penthouse spanned the entire floor—glass on three sides, black stone on the fourth. A single-slab desk veined with fossil-white lines sat before heavy drapes that drank the storm, as the sky poured down in bright arteries of rain.

The Baron didn't rise. Hair silvered at the temples, face flattened by decades of avoiding consequences. His eyes were cold and empty.

A gold cigarette case lay open. He held a pistol.

"Welcome, old friend," the Baron said, voice smooth and mocking.

He fired, knowing it would not be lethal. Glass shattered behind the Revenger as he dove over the desk, shadows sweeping with him. The Baron laughed.

"Yes, yes—use your power. Show me how the shadows obey you."

The Revenger commanded the shadows to coil around the Baron, but they hesitated, then turned against him.

"The shadows belong to me," the Baron scoffed. "And so do you."

With a flick of his wrist, the Baron raised the Revenger high, mockery gleaming in his gaze. "Nothing happens in this town without my say-so. What happened to you, your wife, your home …"

The Revenger felt the weight of those words—faces, flames, screams flooding back. It was all too familiar. The Baron dropped him, leaving him dazed on the floor.

"Pity you still don't understand," the Baron said, feigned concern dripping from every syllable. "At the end, it doesn't matter. It's time for you to go."

The Baron lowered his pistol, confidence radiating from him, convinced he had stripped the Revenger of his power.

In that moment, the Revenger's memory flooded with fragments – the murder, the fire, the loss, and he recognized that the Baron was at the heart of it all. Most prominently, he remembered the face of his wife.

"Remember," he whispered, drawing on her strength. Her strength.

Where there had been shadow, now there was light.

Brilliant beams shot from the Revenger's limbs, overtaking the darkness, blinding the Baron, and stripping the shadows from him.

Commanding both light and shadow now, he allowed the darkness to envelop him once more. The Baron, blinded and burned, collapsed to his knees in disbelief.

"How?!" he stammered, fear creeping into his voice for the first time.

The Revenger grinned, feeling the surge of power. "Pity that you'll never know. It's time for you to go."

Black tendrils curled around the Baron, lifting him off the ground. The Revenger hurled him through the shattered window. The Baron screamed all the way down, his body splashing onto the wet pavement below.

As the Revenger stepped into the rain-soaked night, he felt the burden lift. The sirens wailed behind him; an echo of the chaos left in his wake. But he kept moving forward, embracing the freedom of the world ahead.

He disappeared into the storm, a shadow no longer afraid of the dark.

15

YOUR SIN WILL SET ME FREE

Dawn.

The sky guttered in a half-hearted gray, streetlights still holding their posts long after the night had bled out. Rain came in increments—a fine mist, a sputter, a breathless anticipation before the next downpour.

The Tribune newsstand was the locus, its plastic awning humped and sweating, the day's edition stacked in uneven, rain-laced towers. Each paper glared up, front page angling for the eyes of the first to care.

When the first commuter stumbled from the F train, coat collar already defeated by the weather. He paused at the curb, squinted at the top headline, and blinked twice:

REVENGER TOPPLES SYNDICATE

The font was a size larger than usual, as if to slap the city awake. The man—mid-thirties, hair engineered to resist disaster, fingers nicotine-yellow at the tips—grabbed a paper, flicked it open with ease. He scanned the byline. Kane, E. Good. The only reporter he trusted not to sugarcoat the rot.

Behind him, the morning gathered bodies. Two construction workers from Stanton huddled under a shared umbrella, their boots tracking mud. They grabbed a single copy and bent over it, reading in tandem.

Eleanor's article took three-quarters of the front page, bordered by a blow-up photo of the Baron's private office, its glass walls reduced to a cage.

No blood in the shot, but the implication of violence was louder than sirens. The lede was vintage Kane: clipped, merciless, unafraid of the truth.

"The last criminal king of Manhattan fell last night. For decades, The Syndicate wrote its own laws, bought its own justice. In the end, it was not the NYPD, nor the city's own Bureau, but a single man who dragged the Baron's empire into the light."

Next to the rack, a kid no older than sixteen swept the puddles out from under his hot dog cart, shoes wrapped in shopping bags. He eyed the headlines, then snatched a copy when the owner wasn't looking. He hunched over it, his mouth moving in a silent rehearsal of the story.

After a moment, he looked up and told the nearest stranger, "I saw that guy once. The Revenger. He jumped off the Bridge, landed on a garbage truck, kept going."

The stranger—a woman in a close cropped hairdo, her face already resigned to the day—shrugged. "You believe everything you read?"

The kid grinned.

A battered Chrysler with a broken muffler rolled up to the curb, its driver's window cranked just enough to keep the rain off the upholstery. The man inside—mustache, aviator glasses, badge clipped to his pocket—glanced at the stand, then at the clusters of people reading the paper. He killed the engine.

"Gimme three," he said. "One for the boss, one for the wife, one for the dog."

The owner laughed. "Your dog reads?"

Eleanor Kane woke to the sound of her own name being mispronounced on the radio. She checked her watch, then the blinking light on her answering machine. Three messages from her editor, one from her mother, two from sources with numbers she recognized but would not call back.

She rolled out of bed, lit a cigarette, and scanned the city through the window. Already the rain was lessening, the sky brightening by increments.

She reread her own words on the front page, scribbling changes in her mind she wished she'd made, then let herself feel something close to satisfaction. Not pride, exactly. Just the relief of a job done well—and done before anyone else could.

"The man the press calls the Revenger remains unidentified. Eyewitnesses describe him as a ghost—moving through the city's veins with impossible speed, favoring the broken and the lost. The Tribune reached out to several former Syndicate members for comment. Only one replied from an undisclosed hospital bed: 'He's not human. He's the city, come to collect.'"

By eight in the morning, the line at the stand was ten deep. Some came for the story, some for the hope, most for the ritual. The owner barked at a pair of kids trying to pinch the sports section, then grinned when they gave him the finger and ran.

Later, Father Elias prepared the chapel the way he prepared his soul: not by addition but by subtraction. He killed the overheads, leaving the sanctuary in the benediction of colored glass and the dull gold haze creeping through the east windows.

He shuffled down the central aisle, his cassock trailing over old wax. The votive stand groaned under his weight. He struck a match, then another—each candle, then the next, each a headstone for a name writtenin the ledger, a life bent or warped in the city's endless self-devouring.

The doors were locked, but a draft wormed through the cracks, rattling hymnals in their racks. Rain tapped at the stained glass, drawing streaks through the saints' faces and making the colors crawl across the pews.

He opened his Bible—the real one, with the soft leather cover. The passage was bookmarked.

"Vengeance is mine, saith the Lord."

He whispered it once. Then again, softer, as if the echo could heal him.

Elias closed eyes. He remembered faces, so many faces.

He remembered the woman who'd lost her child to the Baron's crew, who'd begged for absolution for the rage she felt every time she saw a uniform. He remembered the men who'd come to him only after, when the city's engines had already chewed up everything but the guilt.

He remembered a kid named Jack, too.

Before the world turned him inside out.

Elias rubbed his scalp, the gray stubble rasping beneath his palm. His fingers lingered at his throat, where the collar. He unclipped it, set it on the altar, and stared at it—white plastic, dirty at the edges grimy, light as nothing, heavy as a life.

He got to his knees, old bones clicking, then leaned forward until his forehead touched the rail.

He stayed there until his back ached, then shifted to a sitting position, gazing at the candles. In the silence, the only sound was a drip of water from the leak over the third pew, and the distant wail of a cop car speeding toward a place nobody wanted to go. Later, when he locked up, he saw a new version of the painted silhouette of the Revenger, sprayed across the street from the church, on a collapsing wall, by Rook and Echo.

That evening, in a garage three stories below the apartment ruins where the city had last believed him dead. The lights snapped on in sequence, each tube a stab of cold fluorescence, each one stuttering before it held.

The Stutz Blackhawk squatted in its stall, paint wet-black and stitched with the memory of hundreds of bullet scars, each patched but never quite hidden.

He almost remembered his name.

But the memories could wait. The Syndicate was finished, but evil persisted, and new players would surely seek to take their place. He was the Revenger, now and forever.

He climbed inside the Stutz, hands on the wheel, and looked up at his own face in the rearview. He turned the key. The engine coughed before settling into a predatory idle. The stink of gasoline flooded the cabin. He drove out slowly.

At the first stoplight, he saw her: Ashes, the one-eyed cat.

She sat in the gutter, soaked, one ear gone, a constellation of fresh pink scars. She watched the Stutz with a contempt only animals could summon. When the light flipped, she leapt onto the hood, tail high. The Revenger didn't stop. He kept the car in gear, letting it roll, but his eyes met hers through the glass. For a second, neither blinked.

Then the cat meowed, mouth wide, and vanished over the fender.

He turned on the radio. Static, then the ghost of an AM preacher: "...and when you walk through the valley of death, you fear no evil, for you are the evil that makes the valley run..."

He switched it off.

"No Holy Ghost for the devout," he said, almost a prayer.

And the Revenger drove on.